CHRISTMAS
IN THE FOREST

CHRISTMAS IN THE FOREST

by Marion Dane Bauer

illustrated by Diane Dawson Hearn

Holiday House / New York

For Brannon Drake Bauer,
with love
M. D. B.

For Marion Dane Bauer,
with best wishes
D. D. H.

Library of Congress Cataloging-in-Publication Data
Bauer, Marion Dane.
Christmas in the forest / by Marion Dane Bauer; illustrated by
Diane Dawson Hearn. — 1st ed.
p.   cm.
Summary: After Cat is accidentally shut outdoors on a cold, dark
Christmas Eve, she makes a promise to Mouseling in order to share
his warm bed.
ISBN 0-8234-1371-3 (reinforced)
[1. Cats—Fiction.   2. Mice—Fiction.   3. Christmas—Fiction.]
I. Hearn, Diane Dawson, ill.   II. Title.
PZ7.B3262Ch   1998   97-41952   CIP   AC
[E]—dc21

Contents

1. Christmas Schmistmas

Christmas Eve.

The house breathed spice.

Presents peeked

from every hiding place.

Under the shining tree,

a manger waited for the baby.

Christmas Eve.

Everyone was happy.

Everyone was excited.

Everyone was happy and excited.

But not Cat.

"Christmas, schmistmas," Cat hissed.

"My children forgot all about me."

And they had.

They forgot to scratch Cat.
They forgot to brush Cat.
They even forgot to feed Cat
her flaked tuna.
"Please!" she mewed.
"Please, please, please!"
But no one heard.

So when the children opened
the door, Cat ran outside.
"I am running away," she called.
"Come and get me!"
The boy did not see.
The girl did not hear.
"No Santa yet!" they said.
And they shut the door.

Cat stood for a long time
staring at the closed door.
Then she pulled a paw out
of the snow and began to walk.
What could she do but go?
Where could she go
but to the cold,
to the cold, dark,
to the cold, dark, cruel forest?

2. What Is Christmas?

Cat sat alone by the frozen pond.

She was cold.

She was cranky, too.

From the M on her forehead

to the last stripe on her tail,

Cat was cranky and cold.

"At least," she said,

"Christmas will not come

to the forest."

"Christmas?" squeaked a small voice.

It came from a hollow log.

"What is Christmas?"

Cat glared at the log.

"Everyone knows about Christmas,"

she growled.

"I know about nuts and seeds,"
answered the small voice.
"I know about warm nests.
And Mama Mouse has told me
about snow and wind and ice.
But she has not said one word
about Christmas."
Mama Mouse! Cat licked her lips.
What luck!

She was talking
to a tender mouseling.
Mouseling might taste better
than flaked tuna.
Especially for a cat
who was cranky and cold.
"Dear little Mouseling," she said.
"Come out where I can see you.
I will tell you all about Christmas."

"Please, Mama!"
  the small voice cried.
"May I go?
  I am big and brave.
  I am not afraid of Christmas."
"You may not
  be afraid of Christmas,"
  Mama Mouse answered.
"But you had better be afraid
  of that mean, old cat."
Mean? Old? Cat twitched her tail.
  She was a fine, young cat.
  And besides,
  she was always nice to her dinner.

"Come, little one," she called again.
"I will tell you about special foods.
  I will tell you about shining trees.
  I will tell you about presents.
  Don't you want to hear?"

"No!" Mama Mouse cried.

But Mouseling did.

He popped out of the log.

He landed between Cat's paws.

3. Delicious!

"Oh, oh, oh!" chattered Squirrel.

"My, my, my! Don't, don't, don't!"

"Please, Cat!" whistled Bird.

"Pretty please!"

"Watch out, Mouseling!"

Rabbit whispered.

Mama Mouse peeked out of the log.

"Don't eat my dear little Mouseling,"

she begged.

"Why not?" Cat asked.

And Cat licked Mouseling.

The lick began

with his pointy pink nose.

It ended with his pointy pink tail.

"Because, because, because,"

Squirrel chattered.

"His fur would tickle your throat."

"Because," Bird whistled,
"his bones would catch
    in your teeth."
"Because," Rabbit whispered,
"his tail would taste
    like an old rubber band."
"Because," Mama Mouse cried,
"he is my baby!"

"I am sure Mouseling's fur would
slide down my throat," Cat said.
"His bones would
not hurt my teeth.
His tail would be easy to chew.
And," she asked,
"what could be more tasty?"

Then she licked Mouseling again.

This lick began

with his pointy pink tail.

It ended with his pointy pink nose.

"Delicious," she said.

She began to nibble his whiskers.

"Cat," Mouseling squeaked.

"You promised!

You promised

to tell me about Christmas."

Cat stopped.

"Did I promise?" she asked.

"You promised!" everyone cried.

Cat sighed. "Then I must," she said.

"We cats always keep our promises."

"Hurray!" everyone shouted.

"Cat will tell Mouseling

about Christmas!"

For they knew cats are polite.
Even cold and cranky cats.
They do not eat and talk
at the same time.
"Tell Mouseling
about special foods, foods, foods,"
Squirrel chattered.
"Tell him about shining trees,"
Bird whistled.
"Tell him about presents,"
Rabbit whispered.
"Cat is the only one
who knows about Christmas,"
Mama Mouse squeaked.
"Cat is the only one!"
everyone cheered.
Cat purred.

But before she could say a word,

a mound of snow trembled.

It shivered.

It shook.

There was a rumbling growl.

There was a grumbling roar.

And Bear burst out of her den!

4. The Most Special Food

"HOW!" roared Bear.

"DARE!" roared Bear.

"YOU!" roared Bear.

"YOU WOKE ME UP!"

Squirrel and Bird and Rabbit
scurried and flew
and hopped away.
Even Mama Mouse hid.
But Cat did not move.
She wrapped her paw
around Mouseling.
She glared at Bear.

"You are spoiling
my Christmas story,"
she hissed. "Go back to bed!"
Bear rubbed her eyes.

She glared at Cat.

"Christmas?" she asked.

"What is Christmas?"

"Christmas," Cat told her,

"is special foods.

Christmas is shining trees.

Christmas is—"

"Special foods?" Bear asked.

She stepped closer to Cat.

"Special foods?"

Bear said again.

She sniffed Cat.

The sniff began with the M
on Cat's forehead.

It ended with the last stripe
on her tail.

"You smell cranky and cold,"
  Bear said.
"But you must be
  the most special food of all."
  And she licked Cat.
  The lick began
  with the last stripe on Cat's tail.
  It ended with the M
  on her forehead.
"Delicious," Bear said.

5. *The Christmas Baby*

"Oh," Cat said.

"My," Cat said.

"Don't!" Cat said.

She even let go of Mouseling.

Mouseling ran to his mother.

Cat stared into Bear's

small, mean eyes.

She stared into Bear's

large, mean mouth.

"You do not understand," she said.

"Christmas is about the baby."

"The baby?" Bear asked.

"The baby?" Bear said again.

Then she lifted her head.

She sniffed the air.

And she stumbled back to her den.

"Good, good, goodness,"
　Squirrel chattered.
"What a surprise!"
　Bird flew to a bush
　beside Bear's den.
"Bear is already sleeping,"
　Bird whistled.
"Come look! Everyone come!"
　Rabbit was the first
　to reach the den.
"How wonderful!" Rabbit whispered.
"How fine!"
"How wonderful and fine!"
　everyone said.
　For snuggled against Bear,
　warm and sweet and new,
　lay a naked, pink cub.

"The Christmas baby!"
Squirrel said.
"Surely not," Cat said.
"How can it be?
Didn't you know?"
she told them all.
"The Christmas baby is special."

Mama Mouse looked
at the new cub.
She looked at Mouseling.
She looked at Cat.
"All babies are special," she said.
And she kissed
Mouseling's pointy pink nose.

For a long time,

Cat said nothing.

She just looked at the new cub.

She looked at Mouseling.

She looked at the sky,

which would soon be dark.

And her eyes grew round and soft.

For Cat had once had

babies of her own.

And she had loved them fiercely.

"You are right," she said
to Mama Mouse at last.
"All babies *are* special."
Then she leaned close to Mouseling.
But she did not lick.
She did not nibble.
She did not bite.
She kissed his pointy pink nose.

6. Especially at Christmas

A cold moon rose above the trees.

Squirrel and Bird and Rabbit,

Mama Mouse and Mouseling

went to their beds.

Only Cat stayed,

alone by the frozen pond.

She pulled one cold paw

out of the snow.

Then the other.

In the morning

her boy and girl would miss her.

They would open the door and call.

And she would go home.

Until then, the night would be long.

Mouseling spoke

from the hollow log.

"Our nest is warm," he said.

"Could we, Mama?"

"You are so young, little one,"
  Mama Mouse said.

"You do not understand."

"I do understand," Mouseling said.

"Cat is cold."

Cat said nothing. She just waited.

Mama Mouse peeked out of the log.

She looked at Cat for a long time.

Then, at last, she nodded.
"Only you must promise . . . ,"
she said sternly.
Cat's stomach rumbled.
Then she thought about
fur in her throat.
She thought about
bones in her teeth.
She thought about a tail
like an old rubber band.

"I promise," she answered.

"I promise not to eat anyone at all."

And, of course,

cats always keep their promises.

Especially at Christmas!